This copy of

THE OUTER SPACE JOKE BOOK!

belongs to

_____

Other Red Fox *joke books*

THE SMELLY SOCKS JOKE BOOK
by Susan Abbott

THE EVEN SMELLIER SOCKS JOKE BOOK
by Karen King

THE BULLYBUSTERS JOKE BOOK
by John Byrne

SANTA'S CHRISTMAS JOKE BOOK
by Katie Wales

THE GOOD EGG YOLK BOOK by Katie Wales

BEST BROWNIE JOKES by Brownies

BEST CUB JOKES by Cub Scouts

THE SCHOOL RULES JOKE BOOK
by Karen King

THE MILLENNIUM JOKE BOOK
by Sue Mongredien

THE FISH 'N' CHIPS JOKE BOOK by Ian Rylett

AMAZING ANIMAL JOKES by John Hegarty

THE FAT CAT JOKE BOOK by Susan Abbot

THE NUTTY INTERNET JOKE BOOK
by John Byrne

THE FUNNIEST JOKE BOOK
IN THE WORLD EVER

THE FARTY JOKE BOOK by
U. Smell

THE OUTER SPACE JOKE BOOK!

For Toni

A RED FOX BOOK : 0099413159

First published in Great Britain by Red Fox
an imprint of Random House Children's Books

PRINTING HISTORY
Red Fox original 2002

3 5 7 9 10 8 6 4 2

Papers used by Random House Children's Books are natural,
recyclable products made from wood grown in sustainable forests.
The manufacturing processes conform to the environmental regulations
of the country of origin.

Set in 12/13 Century Schoolbook
Red Fox Books are published by Random House Children's Books,
61-63 Uxbridge Road, London W5 5SA,
a division of The Random House Group Ltd,
in Australia by Random House Australia (Pty) Ltd,
20 Alfred Street, Milsons Point, Sydney, NSW 2061, Australia,
in New Zealand by Random House New Zealand Ltd,
18 Poland Road, Glenfield, Auckland 10, New Zealand,
and in South Africa by Random House (Pty) Ltd,
Endulini, 5A Jubilee Road, Parktown 2193, South Africa

THE RANDOM HOUSE GROUP Limited Reg. No. 954009

A CIP catalogue record for this book is available from the British Library.

Printed and bound in Great Britain by Bookmarque Ltd, Croydon, Surrey

www.kidsatrandomhouse.co.uk

Greetings Earthlings!

C3-Hoho and Laugh2D2 here – the funniest robots in outer space (although we don't actually spend much time in space – most of our time is spent in the repair shop, 'cos we've split our sides laughing!)

We've collected all of the greatest gags in the galaxy for you . . . unfortunately a big nasty space villian with a black helmet and breathing problems stole them from us, so you'll have to make do with this lot instead . . . at least until this book gets a sequel!

May the Farce be with you . . .

What did Fred Flintstone say when he met a Hutt?
"Jabba Dabba Doo."

What do you call a droid who spends all his time on the internet?
E-threepio.

What do droids write at the end of letters?
Yours tin-cerely.

This is a letter to let you know I'm tin-king of you...

What steps should you take if you are attacked by a space monster?
Long ones in the opposite direction.

What's much more dangerous than a light sabre?
A heavy sabre.

Why did the space villians go to the pub?
They wanted to play Darths.

What do you say to a space monster who's having trouble sleeping?
May the snores be with you.

Who's the clumsiest space hero in the galaxy?
Bananaskin Skywalker.

What's Dracula's favourite space movie?
The Vampire Strikes Back.

I'm a space vampire I only travel to full moons!

Who's the laziest heroine in the galaxy?
Princess Layabout.

What do space villians play during the summer?
Phantom tennis.

Can robots stand on their heads?
Yes – but they have to take them off first.

Arrgh!
My head's
fallen off!
whoever made
me really put
his foot in it!

"Mummy, mummy – the other robots say
I'm just a clockwork toy."
*"Nonsense, dear – they're just trying to
wind you up."*

What do you get if your cross Anakin
Skywalker with Indiana Jones?
Raiders of The Lost Darth.

Which planet is covered in lots of little
drawings?
Tattoo-ine.

Which city has the most robots?
Electri-city.

What do you get if you stick a space
knight in a photocopier?
Obi-Two Kenobi.

Who's the biggest celebrity in outer
    space?
Star2D2.

Which space hero is always sunbathing?
Tan Solo.

What do you get if you cross Darth Vader
    with a toad?
Star Warts.

May the
warts
be with
you!

What do you get if you hang your
    spaceship on a clothesline?
An unidentified drying object.

What do you call an alien with six ears?
*You don't need to call at all – he can hear
    you even if you whisper.*

C3-Hoho: The other robots are saying
   I'm mad!
Laugh2D2: Nonsense! You've just got a
   screw loose.

Laugh2D2: My batteries are flat. Can
   you help me?
C3-Hoho: Yes – but I'm afraid I'm going
   to have to charge you.

Laugh2D2: My batteries are still flat.
C3-Hoho: What shape are they supposed
to be?

What do you get if you cross James Bond
with Star Wars?
Luke Spywalker.

"There's a one-legged robot outside."
"Tell him to hop it."

What do Jedi Werewolves say to one another?
"May the furs be with you."

Why does Luke Skywalker's planet have two suns?
Just Luke-y, I guess.

Where do space explorers go at 11am?
For their E.T. break.

What's a space villain's favourite game?
Conquers.

What do you call a space explorer with a
cold?
A *hoarse-tronaut.*

What do space pilots play when they're
bored?
Ring-X-wing-a-Roses.

What do you get from the space monsters
on the Ice planet?
Frostbite.

M-May the
F-froze be
w-with you..

Knock, knock.
Who's there?
Luke.
Luke who?
*Luke out! There's a bunch of
stormtroopers chasing you!*

Knock, knock.
Who's there?
Jabba.
Jabba who?
*Jabba screwdriver I can borrow? The
   bell's not working.*

What do you call a space knight in a tent?
Obi-Wan Canopy.

Where do you find the most alien scouts?

Tent-ooine!

When was the first tennis match in space
   played?
A lawn time ago in a galaxy far away.

Who was the first robot tennis champion?
Tin Henman.

Why is Wimbledon still better for tennis
than outer space?
It's got a lot more atmosphere.

Why was the space knight fat?
He'd been Force fed.

I'M a spaceburger!

may the sauce be with you!

"Do you think space movies are as exciting when you watch them on the television?"
"Yes – *but it's much more comfortable to sit on the sofa.*"

Why did the robot drink a pint of grease before it went to bed?
It wanted to wake up oily in the morning.

Why does a space rocket roar?
You would too, if your bottom was on fire.

What do you get if you cross a space
knight with a detective?
The Police Force.

I'M a police robot...

Oil-o, Oil-o, Oil-o...

C3-Hoho: What do Hutts have that no
other creature in the universe has?
Laugh2D2: Baby Hutts.

C3-Hoho: What's the space robot motto?
Laugh2D2: "If at first you don't succeed,
droid, droid again"

What do you get if your cross Miss Piggy
   with the leader of Naboo?
Queen Hamidala.

Who's the most famous cowboy in outer
   space?
The Clone Ranger.

Which space station cost the most money
   to build?
The Debt Star.

What do you get if you drive a space
monster down the motorway?
Car Wars.

Where do robots go for a swim?
In the Sea-3PO.

LUKE: Doctor, doctor – I was fixing one of
the robots and I swallowed the spanner.
DOCTOR: Are you choking?
LUKE: No, I'm serious.

Where are the best shops in outer space?
In the Darth Mall.

Which alien has the worst eyesight?
Jar Jar Blinks.

What goes Mooz Mooz?
A spaceship flying backwards.

What do you call a parrot with a light sabre?
Anakin Sky-squawker.

Who's the scariest alien in outer space?
The Naboo-gie man.

when do space creatures get scared?

once in a boo moon!

Why was the space villian rushed to hospital?
He'd had a Darth Attack.

How do you start a Pod Race?
"One-two-pea . . . go!"

My favourite race is the human race... Delicious!

What do you say to an alien viking?
May the Norse be with you.

What do you call a space monster in a
sauna?
Jabba the Hot.

Who's the tubbiest bounty hunter in the
  galaxy?
Boba Fatt.

Knock, knock.
Who's there?
Yoda and Leia.
Yoda and Leia who?
Stop yodelling and open the door!

What do you find on a space librarian's
  desk?
The Returns of the Jedi.

What do space villains inhale when they
  have a blocked nose?
Darth Vapours.

What do you get if you cross a chicken
  with Darth Vader?
Fowl play.

C3-Hoho: What do you call an astronaut
  with a box of sandwiches?
Laugh2D2: A rocket luncher.

C3-Hoho: Why did the alien fill his
  spaceship with lampshades?
Laugh2D2: He wanted to reach light
  speed.

Why did the robot put prune juice in his
  battery pack?
He wanted to keep going all night.

What do you give a lazy droid?
A kick in the Ro-butt.

What do you get if you cross a space
  villain with a restaurant?
Darth Waiter.

What kind of car does an 800-year-old
   space knight drive?
A Toy-Yoda.

Why is a robot designer never lonely?
Because he's always making new friends.

Which droid wrote *Treasure Island*?
Robot Louis Stephenson.

What do you call a person who invites an
   alien to dinner?
The main course.

Why was the baby spaceship crying?
It missed its mothership.

Why is a
Spoiled
baby like
an old
robot?

They're
both got
lots of
rattles.

What goes ha-ha-ha . . . bonk?
A robot laughing its head off!

Why did the robot chicken cross the road?
To get to the other droid.

How do you know if an alien has three
eyes?
Ask to see his eye-eye-eye D.

Knock, knock.
Who's there?
Han.
Han who?
Han me the key, I'll open the door myself!

"Have you seen that new science fiction film, *Escape from the Prison Planet*?"
"No – it hasn't been released yet."

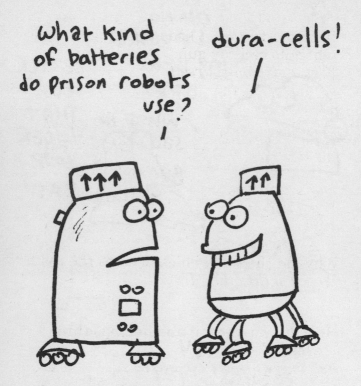

ALIEN: Tell me the truth, doc – will I be able to fly straight after my operation?

DOCTOR: Of course you will.

ALIEN: Great – I could never afford a spaceship before!

What do you get if you cross ten aliens
   with Humpty Dumpty?
Ten green bottoms hanging on a wall.

"Doctor, doctor – I keep thinking I'm the
   handle of a ray gun."
"Get a grip on yourself."

C3-Hoho: What comes out of a really
   sleepy alien's gun?
Laugh2D2: A lazy-er beam.

C3-Hoho: What do you get when you cross a robot with a moon rock?
Laugh2D2: An as-droid.

What do you get if you cross a spaceman with a police officer?
Fuzz Lightyear.

What do you get
if you cross a bee
with a spaceman?

Buzz
Lightyear!

Where do they throw criminal aliens?
In the Jar Jar Clink.

Which alien is the best at golf?
Jabba the Putt.

What was Jabba the Putt's best golf
　　score?
A black hole in one.

Where do space dogs bury their bones?
In black holes.

What's got four ears, eight legs and two
　　bottoms?
A robot with spare parts.

What's got four ears, eight legs, two bottoms but only one hand?
A robot with spare parts but no idea where the second-hand shop is.

What do you get if you cross an alien with a dog?
No more visits from the postman.

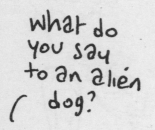

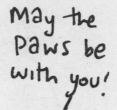

What do alien boy scouts learn to tie?
Jedi Knots.

What did one robot say to the other
robot?
"I've taken a shine to you."

What did the other robot's boyfriend say
to the first robot?
*"If you don't get out of here I'll soon
polish you off."*

What do you call a space monster who
    talks too much?
Blabba the Hutt.

How do Australians travel through outer
    space?
In didgeridoo-F.Os.

what do you call an
alien sitting on a wall?

HUMP-E.T.
DUMP-E.T.!

Humpty Dumpty sat on the wall
And suddenly fell from his place.
He landed on top of an alien blob,
Now he's bouncing around outer space.

Have you heard the one about the alien
  who polishes robots?
Yes – it's a story of rags to switches.

What's the smelliest planet in space?
Na-pooh.

What should you remember before you
  step into an alien spacecraft?
Not to get carried away.

what do you
call a dog in
a spaceship?

Pup, pup
and
away...

"Doctor, doctor – I keep thinking I'm one
  of the cat people from Planet Zzong!"
"How long has this been going on?"
"Since I thought I was one of the kitten
  people from Planet Zzong."

Why do space explorers go bald?
They don't get much fresh hair.

EARTHLING: Ugh! What a horrible looking
   creature!
ALIEN: I know you are, but I like you
   anyway.

MIRROR, MIRROR
on the wall...

Arrgh!
If you think
I'm staying
to look at
that mug,
you must be
cracked!

FIRST ALIEN: I'm bored. Let's race our
   spaceships.
SECOND ALIEN: What's the point? The
   spaceships are bound to beat us.

What do the seven dwarf aliens sing?
"U.F.O., U.F.O., it's off to work we go. . ."

FIRST ALIEN: Where on Planet Earth did your sister land her spaceship?
SECOND ALIEN: Alaska.
FIRST ALIEN: Don't bother, I'll ask her myself.

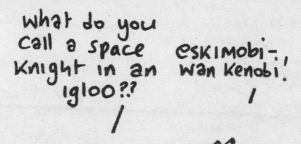

EARTHLING: Why are you aliens wearing those red spacesuits?

ALIEN: So we can hide in rhubarb.

EARTHLING: But I've never seen aliens hiding in rhubarb.

ALIEN: See? It works!

C3-Hoho: What do you get if you cross an elephant with a spaceship?

Laugh2D2: Great big holes all over the space station.

C3-Hoho: How do alien farmers catch trespassers?

Laugh2D2: With a tractor beam.

Which space villain paints pictures in his
   spare time?
Art Vader.

Which alien likes to breed rabbits?
Jabba the Hutch.

Which space hero has the sharpest teeth?
Piranha-kin Skywalker.

What name did Little Bo Peep use when
   she went into space?
Queen Lamb-idala.

Which droid is always buying apples for the teacher?
C-creepio.

Why was the robot no good at dancing?
He had two left feet.

How does Harrison Ford Dance?

Solo, Solo, Quick Quick, Solo!

How do polite robots sit at the dinner table?
Bolt upright.

Where do aliens get honey?
From Obi-Wan Keno-bees.

Why did the robot pump himself up?
Because his batteries were flat.

arrgh! I've swallowed a balloon!

Well, you always DID have an inflated opinion of yourself!

C3-Hoho: Why didn't the alien have a pedigree dog?
Laugh2D2: He preferred moon-grels.

What do you call a fairytale about a
  princess and a droid?
Beauty and the Bleep.

What was the robot's favourite Christmas
  song?
Rusty the Snowman.

Who eats all the marmalade in outer
  space?
Queen Jamidala.

What's got a red face, horns and is only
two foot high?
Darth Small.

How do you make a robot Christmas
pudding?
With lots of droid fruit.

What happened to the robot who fooled
around with a laser sword?
He was cut and droid.

Why did Princess Leia lose her job at the
bakery?
*Because they kept finding her hair in
buns.*

What's the droid's motto?
"Look before you bleep."

what's the
spaceship's
motto?

"if at first
you don't succeed,
fly, fly again!"

What do space giants say?
"Fee-fi-U.F.O.-fum!"

What do you get if you cross a robot with
a teddy bear?
Tinny the Pooh.

ALIEN: How much is a return spaceflight?
STARSHIP CAPTAIN: Where to?
ALIEN: Back here, of course.

"Doctor, doctor – I keep thinking I'm an
  alien."
"Nonsense – you just need a holiday."
"You're right – I've heard Mars is nice
  this time of year . . ."

What's big and grey and terrorises the
  galaxy?
The Elephantom Menace.

What do robots sing when they get
  impatient?
"Wire we waiting?"

What do you get if you cross a robot with
  a chicken?
A battery hen.

SPACE EXPLORER:
  I've been flying
  around the galaxy
  for fifty years.
ALIEN: Really? You'd
  think you'd have
  reached where you
  were going by now.

What do you find in an alien fridge?
Jar Jar drinks.

What wears a long black dress and goes
round the galaxy shouting
"Exterminate!"?
Queen Amildalek.

What do you say to a space hero who's
going to hospital?
"May the nurse be with you."

What do you say to a space hero on his
   birthday?
"Force he's a jolly good fellow."

what did
Luke Skywalker
get for his
birthday?

an ewok-man.

C3-Hoho: Why did the robot stick a
   magnet on its nose?
Laugh2D2: It wanted to make itself
   more attractive.

What is the space pirate's favourite
   saying?
Yoda-ho-ho and a bottle of rum.

What time was it when the space monster
  swallowed the Prime Minister?
Ate P.M.

What's got a long neck, a beak and a laser
  sword?
Obi-swan Kenobi.

What do you call a Gaul in a spacesuit?
An Asterix-naut.

Who's the greatest spy in the galaxy?
U.F.O-07.

Where do space heroes plant potatoes?
In a Force Field.

C3-Hoho: What do you call a dog in a spaceship?
Laugh2D2: An astromutt.

who looks after pets in outer space?

Luke Dogwalker!

What's a hungry space hero's favourite time of the day?
Launchtime.

What do alien squirrels eat?
Astronuts.

Do space wizards go to Hogwarts?

no... Starwarts!

What do you get if you cross Star Wars
    with Harry Potter?
A Flying Sorcerer.

"I want to be an astronaut when I grow
    up."
"Gosh, you've got high hopes."

Why does E.T. like omelettes?
Because he's an Eggs-tra Terrestrial.

What did the alien say to the large bottle
   of pop?
"Take me to your Litre."

What did the alien say to the petrol
   pump?
*"Don't stick your finger in your ear when
   I'm talking to you."*

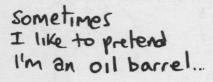

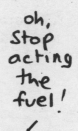

How do robots shave?
With a laser blade.

Which robot always takes the long way round?
R2Detour.

Do robots have brothers?
No, just transistors.

What did the Moon say to the Earth?
"I'm not going around with you any more."

who'd have thought the moon would have a watch?

a lunar-tick.

What's shiny and wears a kilt?
Robot the Bruce.

Why do alien barbers reach Earth before
  any of their friends?
Because they know all the short cuts.

who
ever heard
of a robot
with a hat?

well, my hair's
  getting
  "tin"...

What do you call twin robots?
R2Ditto.

C3-Hoho: Which TV channel do robots
  watch?
Laugh2D2: Beep.Beep.C.

C3-Hoho: Why did the robot have a lid
  on top of his head?
Laugh2D2: Because he was always
  changing his mind.

What do you call a droid that eats lots of chips?
Heavy Metal.

What did the robot have for its tea?
Fish and computer chips.

FIRST SCIENTIST: I thought I told you to take that space creature to the museum.
SECOND SCIENTIST: I did – but now he wants to go to the cinema.

What do you say to a smelly alien on her birthday?
"For cheese a jolly good fellow."

what do you call a space villain who doesn't bath?

Dirt Vader!

What's nasty, breathes heavily and
  charges too much for robot spares?
Parts Vader.

What's the most boring science fiction
  movie?
Snore Wars.

Why did the robot have a light on top of
  his head?
To give him bright ideas.

What is the astronaut's motto?
*"If at first you don't succeed, fly, fly
  again."*

What do you call a group of aliens in their underpants?
Star Trek – the knicks generation.

Why didn't the left-handed alien appear in the space movie?
He wasn't right for the part.

FIRST ALIEN: On my planet, Pluto, it's far too cold to walk and you can't use flying saucers because the engines freeze up.
SECOND ALIEN: So how do you travel about the place?
FIRST ALIEN: By icicle.

What's the smallest planet in the galaxy?
Tatoo-weeny.

Where do you take
a sick space knight?

To
a
force-pital!

Why was the alien crossing his legs?
He was dying to go to the Loo.F.O.

Why didn't the six-armed alien need
petrol in her spaceship?
Because many hands make flight work.

"Doctor, doctor – I come from a planet
way, way up in the sky."
*"So why have you come to see an Earth
doctor like me?"*
"I'm scared of heights."

FIRST ROBOT: Can you tell me if the indicator on my space pod is working?
SECOND ROBOT: Yes, no, yes, no, yes, no, yes, no...

"Doctor, doctor – I keep thinking I'm an alien!"
"Don't worry – my bill will bring you right down to earth."

C3-Hoho: What kind of stories do insects like to read?
Laugh2D2: Sci-ants Fiction.

C3-Hoho: What spaceships do smelly aliens drive?
Laugh2D2: Phew.F.O.s.

Why would Han never betray Luke?
He wouldn't stoop solo.

Where do the smelliest aliens live?
Somewhere in the garlic-sy.

What's E.T.'s favourite TV show?
Phone Home and Away.

What should you sing to an alien who's
just arrived on this planet?
"Happy Earth-day to You."

Do robots like to eat raisins?
*No, but they're very fond of electric
currants.*

Why did the alien policeman always say
"Hello, Hello, Hello"?
Because he had three heads.

what do you get
if you cross a
Spaceknight with
a police
Siren?

OBI-BAH-BI-BAH-
BI-BAH WAN
KENOBI!

When are moon monsters most scary?
When there's an eek-clipse.

What do you call a mummy in a rocket?
Tutankha-moon.

How do aliens go fishing?
With a plan-net.

What kind of fish do they try to catch?
Starfish.

who's the
ocean's scariest
space villain?

Carp
Vader!

What's the worst kind of bait to use for
    starfish?
Earth worms.

What happened to the robot with a sore
  throat?
It had to have its tin-sels out.

Why did the alien army send their
  soldiers to Mars?
*So they could spend the whole day
  Martian up and down.*

Who swings through outer space on a
  creeper?
Starzan.

where can you
find the best wine
  in space?

on the
planet
of the Grapes!

What's smelly, has pointed ears and lives
   on the Starship Enterprise?
Mr Sock.

What did Captain Kirk say when he
   wanted a pet dog?
"Beam me up a Scottie!"

What's green and slimy and tells stories
   with happy endings?
A fairy t-alien.

Did you hear about the alien with
   fourteen arms?
She was handy to have around.

which space
hero has the
most arms?

Hands
Solo!

How does a robot eat his food?
He bolts it down.

FIRST ALIEN: I hear you visited the Paper
  Planet. What was it like?
SECOND ALIEN: Tear-able.

What's black and white and red all over and wants to rule the galaxy?

Darth Paper!

Why did the alien keep metal polish in
  her rocket?
She wanted to rise and shine.

What did the space monster say when it
  saw a rocket landing?
"Oh good – tinned food!"

What do robot scouts sing?
"Tin can, gooley gooley gooley . . ."

C3-Hoho: Where do space monks live?
Laugh2D2: In a moon-astry.

What do space monsters have on their
toast?
Mars-malade.

What's Darth
Maul's favourite
Soup?

The
Phantom
menace-trone !

What did the Dalek say to the chicken?
Eggs-terminate!

What game do space monsters play when
it rains?
Moon-opoly.

What did the astronaut say to the
invisible space monster?
"I haven't seen very much of you lately."

What do you call empty spacesuits?
Astro-noughts.

Why do humans wear space helmets?

'cos there's so much space between their ears!

Why don't space scientists like studying
   moonrocks?
Because that's a very hard subject.

Which side of a spaceship is the safest
   to sit in?
The inside.

Which is the moon monster's least
   favourite day?
Sunday.

What did Planet Earth say to Planet
   Saturn?
"You must give me a ring sometime."

Why did the alien put a mouse in his
   space rocket?
*He wanted to make
   a little go a
   long way.*

What would you call an alien who was born on Mars, lived on Venus and died on Saturn?
Dead.

Which space villain has the most Pokémon cards?
Darth Trader.

C3-Hoho: Which space hero has passed all his music exams?
Laugh2D2: Piano-kin Skywalker.

C3-Hoho: What did the alien say to Robin Hood?
Laugh2D2: May the forest be with you.

What do you call a spaceship with no wings?
An EX-wing fighter.

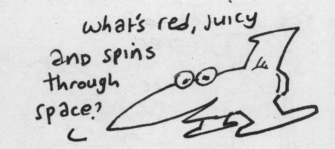

what's red, juicy and spins through space?

a tomato saucer!

Which space knight is always trying to borrow money?
Broke-y-Wan Kenobi.

What is Jabba the Hutt's middle name?
The.

Why is the Millennium Falcon so slow?
*Because it takes a millennium to get
  anywhere.*

What is a space knight's favourite toy?
A yo-yoda.

Why is Han such a loner?
Because he's always solo.

Where does Jabba eat?
Pizza Hutt.

Where does Darth Maul watch TV?
In his Sith-ing room.

What do you get if you cross a space
  knight with a sausage?
Obi-Wan Baloney.

What do you get if you cross an alien with
  a dog?
Jabba the Mutt.

Which alien lives entirely on bubblegum?
Chewie.

C3-Hoho: What is a bull's favourite movie?
Laugh2D2: Steer Wars.

Knock, knock.
Who's there?
Leia.
Leia who?
Leia hand on me and I'll thump you!

Knock Knock!
who's there?
DROID!
DROID who?

DROID to open the door but it's locked!

Knock, knock.
Who's there?
Yoda.
Yoda who?
Yo-da man!

Knock, knock.
Who's there?
Han.
Han who?
Han me the key, I'll open the door myself!

What's evil and jumps the queue at
  science fiction movies?
The FAN-DOM Menace.

which space
movie is all
in verse?

"attack
of the
poems"

What happened when Anakin's left
  indicator switched off?
He had to turn to the dark side.

What do space heroes do when they
   escape from big hairy monsters?
Thank their wookie stars.

How do space heroes fry chinese food?
In an e-wok.

Why is the Millennium Falcon full of
   second-hand clothes?
They are all Han me downs.

What do you get if you cross a space
   knight with a nun?
A Force of Habit.

what do you call a robot nun?

a trans-sister.

Why do space villains blow up planets?
For ALDERAAN reasons.

Where do aliens find work?
The Jabba Centre.

What did one 800-year-old alien say to the
   other 800-year-old alien?
"Yoda one for me!"

What do the Skywalker family do when
   they're annoyed with someone?
They give them dirty lukes.

who's the oldest skywalker?

Granny-kin!

What kind of ticks do you find on the
   moon?
Lunar-ticks.

What kind of bulbs should you plant on
   the sun?
Light bulbs.

Why are scientists always trying to fly to the sun?

So they can have bright ideas!

When is a window like a star?
When it's a skylight.

What kind of poem can you find in outer
    space?
Uni-verse!

How do space cats drink milk?
From flying saucers.

Because
he heard
It was
a `Dessert
planet!

why did the
monster try to
eat
Tatooine?

Why couldn't the astronaut land on the
    moon?
It was already full.

What's the best way to talk to a space
  monster?
Long distance.

What's a Martian's normal eyesight?
20-20-20 vision.

Where does the Martian president live?
In the Greenhouse.

Who starred in the Martian version of
  King Kong?
The Jolly Green Giant.

what do you call
a Twenty foot space
knight that eats
      bananas? Ana-Kong
              Skywalker!

What's the Martian currency?
Greenbacks.

Why shouldn't you sunbathe on Mars?
You'd sink into the melted chocolate.

What is the name of the UN peace troops
on Mars?
Green peace.

Why do Martians have two antennas on
their head?
So they can listen in stereo.

What do
you call a
robot who never
stops watching Tv.?

BBC-3PO!

What's the most popular snack on Mars?
Marsmallows.

Which Bounty Hunter is always making
   mistakes?
BooBoo Fett.

C3-Hoho: Why do space monsters never
   attack Martians?
Laugh2D2: Because they don't like
   eating their greens.

C3-Hoho: What happened to the space
   villain who bought a pet tiger?
Laugh2D2: He got Darth Mauled.

What do you get if you cross a space hero
   with a ghost?
Spook Skywalker.

How do space
Knights fly to
School?

In exam
wing
fighters!

What do you get if your cross an alien
   with a goat?
Jabba the Butt.

Which space knight is always laughing?
Jokey-Wan Kenobi.

Why did the boy become an astronaut?
Because he was no earthly good.

What do astronauts wear to keep warm?
Apollo-neck sweaters.

Where do astronauts leave their
   spaceships?
At parking meteors.

Where do Martians drink beer?
At a mars bar.

How do you get a baby astronaut to sleep?
You rock-et!

which planet
has the most
   babies?

ToT-Tooine!

Where does Dr Who buy his cheese?
At a dalek-atessen.

C3-Hoho: Who is tall, dark and a great
 dancer?
Laugh2D2: Darth Raver.

C3-Hoho: Why did Captain Kirk go into
 the ladies toilet?
Laugh2D2: To boldly go where no man
 has been before!

How does Luke Skywalker get from one
 planet to the other?
Ewoks.

What do you get if you cross a space
   villain with a musketeer?
Darth'agnan.

What is a pig's favourite movie?
Sty Wars.

what do
you call
a pig
with a
lightsabre?

Luke
Stystalker!

Has *Sty Wars* got good special effects?
Yes – but the acting's a bit hammy.

What did one space sausage say to the
   other space sausage?
"May the forks be with you."

what do you call a pig with a laser sword...

an-oink-in skywalker

Which space hero has a hole in his
   middle?
Han Polo.

What do you get if you cross Little Bo
   Peep with an alien?
Jar Jar Blacksheep.

What do Scottish aliens say to each other?
"May the Forth be with you!"

When do space knights play practical
   jokes?
On the Force of April.

Why did the Martian take all his clothes
   off?
He wanted to green and bare it.

What do space knights put in vegetable
  stew?
The re-turnips of the Jedi.

Who's the galaxy's craziest alien?
Jabba the Nutt.

Which space knight has a friend called
  BooBoo?
Yogi-Wan Kenobi.

What's an alien's favourite part of the newspaper?

The star-toons!

Where do space knights store all their junk?
The Attic of the Clones.

In which space movie do classical musicians get hunted down and captured?
The Empire Strikes Bach.

C3-Hoho: What do you call a cat and mouse in outer space?
Laugh2D2: Tom and Jedi.

C3-Hoho: How does Captain Solo wipe his nose?
Laugh2D2: With a Han-kerchief.

what do you call
a robot with a
runny
nose?

R-FLU-D2

Knock, knock.
Who's there?
Leia.
Leia who?
Leia out the red carpet, can't you see I'm a princess?

"Doctor, doctor – I keep thinking I'm a
   space movie."
"When did this start happening?"
"A long time ago in a galaxy far, far away."

"Doctor, doctor – I keep thinking I'm a
   space movie."
"You told me that before."
"I know – this is the sequel."

That's the end
of the book...
see you round!

yeah –
may the
jokes be
with
you!

The NUTTY INTERNET Joke Book

JOHN BYRNE

Do you know who has the best website in the jungle?

* If you're **CRAZY** about computers and **UTTERLY NUTTY** about the **NET** this collection of computer **CRACK-UPS** will have you keeling over at your keyboard. It's chock full of great gags and **ONLINE ONE-LINERS** as well as top tips on where to find the silliest sites and **WACKIEST** web pages. So log on for **LAUGHTER** and lots, lots more! *

0-09-940905-4   £2.99